ANNEMARIE NIKOLAUS

GONE...

– SHORT STORIES –

CONTENT

The Settlement

Three Fiats with the golden flame of the *Guardia di Finanza* printed on their doors were parked in front of his bank this morning. It annoyed bank manager Michele Perini that they were parked directly in front of his door. It made it unmistakeably clear to every passer-by that the financial police were investigating the bank.

Through the glass entrance, he could see the entire lobby. Only two uniformed police officers were hanging around outside his office, meaning the rest were already in the conference room and looking at files.

At one of the counters, there was a customer whose name escaped him. On the opposite wall, Fernando d'Alesi was leaning with his face hidden behind a newspaper – he recognised the heir of the ancient noble family by his ring.

Michele wiped his brow with his handkerchief. Then he folded it again along the creases and entered the bank.

Despite seeming so engrossed, d'Alesi immediately made a beeline for him. "*Direttore*, I've been waiting for an hour. I really must talk to you."

"Please, spare yourself the bother of coming by every morning. As soon as the files have been released, I will contact you. I really am very sorry to delay you; you know that." He left him where he was and hurried towards his office.

One of the police officers standing in front of his office asked, "The young man who waits here for you every day; what does he want?"

"Money. What else do people want from a bank?"

Michele awoke with a yelp.

"*Oddio*, Michele, what are you dreaming about now?!" His wife Carla turned the bedside lamp on, letting out a sigh. "If it's going to carry on like this for the next few nights, I'd rather sleep in the spare room. As if you whimpering like an abandoned kitten wasn't enough, now you're flinging your arms about." She felt for his hand underneath the duvet and squeezed. "Same dream again?"

"She's getting closer every night! I run and run, but I can't get away from her. This time her arms were reaching out towards me. I felt her breath on the back of my neck." He shivered. "And then a great abyss appeared – there was no way out. It was awful! Nothing can save me from her wrath." He wiped his brow, which was covered in sweat. "Maybe I shouldn't eat so much when I come home late."

"Maybe you shouldn't come home late at all."

"Sweetheart, I can't leave my people to deal with the financial police by themselves. That wouldn't be right. Just a few more days; then the nightmare's over. I'm sure no one at the bank was knowingly involved in money laundering."

"Then you should be able to sleep soundly," she retorted. "Anyway, why is it never the magistrate who appears in your dream? Why is it always the old countess who chases you?"

He couldn't answer that. He stared out of the window. In the light of the full moon, Castle Madruzzo sat like a silhouette on top of the hill in the distance. He shivered at the sight of it and pulled the duvet up to his face.

The following week, Michele parked his car in front of the beige walls of Castle Madruzzo. Breathing heavily, he climbed the steep porphyry staircase to the first floor. D'Alesi had restored half of the first floor and fitted a bathroom and heating. The rest of the castle had been uninhabited for a long time.

Hanging on the walls of the staircase were pictures of d'Alesi's noble ancestors: all of them sinister looking paintings, apart from one. Contessa Marcella de Eccher – Fernando d'Alesi's grandmother – wasn't only shown in watercolour as a young girl. Next to that, there was also a portrait photo that had probably been taken shortly before her death. She looked exactly as she appeared in Michele's dreams.

D'Alesi came out of the sitting room. "You look exhausted, *Direttore*. Thank you for making the effort to come by so late."

"Well, at least we won't be disturbed here and can look at the documents in peace and quiet." He laid three stuffed folders on the oak table in the middle of the room. As he opened the clasps, they almost fell apart completely. "Your beloved grandmother was, unfortunately, a little bit disorganised. She simply insisted on her own filing system. That's why I've allowed myself to sort the files before I came."

"The most important thing is that the documents are all complete. Everything else will sort itself out." D'Alesi reached for a pile of roughly-folded forms.

They sat looking at the documents for the numerous stock market dealings the countess had been involved in in the few years before her death until late in the night. Now and again, they looked at each other amazed when they came across a particularly successful speculation.

"It really is fascinating," said Michele eventually. "You'd

be tempted to think your grandmother had a sixth sense about the stock market."

"But what did she end up doing with all that money?" asked d'Alesi.

"Well it's not in our bank."

"But you haven't brought any documents which show she withdrew everything."

"There isn't a bank account the remaining money could be in. Which means it isn't there."

D'Alesi sighed. "We need that money so badly. We have to restore the roof and the tower before the autumn. One more stormy winter and everything will collapse. In any case, it can't be right, *Direttore*. There must be more documents. The ones you've brought with you can't be everything."

"You're most likely right." Michele let his gaze rest on the dark shelving unit in the corner of the room. "But you know yourself that the financial police have turned over every piece of paper three times in the last few weeks. If we had any more documents, they would have been found. And then I'd know about it."

"I doubt it. You can't find something if you don't look for it!"

Michele nodded twice and continued to stare at the shelves. "Have you looked everywhere here?" He knew that his question was pointless and smiled when d'Alesi didn't answer. He was going to be busy in the next few days and wouldn't turn up at the bank.

As he left the castle later on, he realised that from the way the dead countess' photo was hanging, her gaze followed him as he went down the stairs. By the time he got to the door, a cold sweat had broken out on his forehead. He pulled out his handkerchief, unfolded it with shaking hands and wiped his brow. He didn't manage to fold it again. So, he balled it up, stuffed it in his trouser pocket and opened the heavy door with a groan.

The next morning, Carla found him dead in his bed.

"Heart attack," concluded the doctor and shook his head. "And he was so healthy!"

Whilst clearing out Michele's desk at home after the funeral, Carla came across a thin folder labelled "Marcella de Eccher" ...

THE END

The Necklace

"If only I could always hold you in my arms like this!" Robert buried his face in Sonja's long hair. "I'd give anything," he whispered into her neck.

Sonja smiled at his reflection. "It's beautiful." She stroked the pearl necklace that Robert had just placed around her neck.

Then she gently pulled away from him. "Don't be stupid! If you got a divorce, you would lose the factory. It doesn't matter to me that I'm only your lover." She turned around and gave him a kiss. "And now I've finally got the job as the representative for Asia with your help! Now we can spend whole days together." She kissed him again. "Your wife will never find out why you're suddenly flying to Singapore all the time."

"Don't bet on it! She's always checking up on me. Elena's thought for a long time that the only reason I married her was for her money!"

"Well, she's not entirely wrong!"

"That's not true!" Robert protested vehemently. "I've always cared about her. Even in nursery school. She even beat up her older brothers for me. She protected me from everything. How could I not care about her?" He pulled Sonja to him again and smiled. "But you're the one I really love. I'd give up everything for you."

Sonja grimaced. "You're repeating yourself, darling. Come

on, let's raise a glass for my birthday and then I'm throwing you out. You've got the concert to go to with your wife."

After Robert had left, Sonja picked up the telephone, breathing a sigh of relief. "It's me." Her fingers played with the pearl necklace as she listened. "No," she said, " as usual, he was in a hurry. But he told me again how he wants to be with me forever."

She frowned as the person on the other end replied. "No," she concluded, "I don't believe that he's actually going to get divorced either."

Elena was waiting in front of the theatre entrance. She'd turned up the shawl collar of her purple faux-fur coat and was warming her hands under her armpits. "Where've you been?" she hissed as Robert hurried towards her. "I've already rung the office three times!"

"Sorry; these dimwits forget how to drive as soon as there's the tiniest snowflake. I always forget that."

"That's not all! Apparently, you've also forgotten to pick up the pearl necklace you ordered."

"What?" Robert stared at her, his eyes wide with shock.

"I was at the jeweller's yesterday and he asked me what was going on with it. He's been waiting a week for you to pick it up."

Robert swore loudly. "What an idiot! He's ruined everything now!"

Elena bit her lip. "What's that supposed to mean? You know exactly how much I detest pearls. Is this your way of gently telling me that I've become an old frump?"

"Oh, Elena!" protested Robert indignantly. "I won't get you a necklace then. Do you always have to argue with me?"

"Well, if you're going to spend my money, please spend it wisely!"

Sonja sat on the park bench with her eyes closed; her face

raised to the spring sun. Footsteps crunched on the gravel behind her. She turned around and smiled at Robert. "How nice that you were able to tear yourself away after all. I'd almost given up waiting. My plane leaves in an hour."

"You're only in the country for one day! Of course I've got time for you. I've waited so long to see you again. Your idea of working in Singapore hasn't helped us at all; just the opposite, in fact!"

"Oh Robert, stop whingeing! Just be happy that I'm here now. And be happy for me that I'm so successful in Singapore. No-one can complain about your recommendation."

"Of course I'm happy about your career." Robert sat next to her and put his arm around her shoulder. "You're amazing, baby. I always knew you could do it. You just needed a springboard and now you've shown everyone. But don't I deserve a reward anyway?"

"For the springboard you gave me?" She kissed him quickly on the cheek. "I love you, isn't that enough? And I think about you even when I'm far away. Your pearls remind me of you every day."

Robert grumbled, frustrated. "No, that's not enough. That's not enough at all. Don't go back to Singapore. I want you all to myself! I'll find a way."

Sonja frowned and looked at him with big eyes. She began to answer but Robert closed her mouth with a lingering kiss.

Sonja sat at her desk in Singapore and stared into the dusk. The wind was blowing the autumn leaves about and the street gradually lit up with the glow of the neon signs.

One of the telephones rang. When she saw the number on the display, a smile spread across her face.

"I'm nearly finished," she answered. "I'll see you in half an hour at Wu-Cheng. Can't wait."

She was just putting her coat on when the office door opened behind her. Robert was standing in the doorway and grinning at her. "Hi, angel. Did I surprise you?"

Sonja gasped. "You did! What are you doing in Singapore all of a sudden?"

"Elena had an accident yesterday. She's dead!

"Wh-what?" uttered Sonja.

Robert took her hands and kissed one finger at a time. "Elena's dead," he repeated. "Now we don't have any problems anymore."

"What are you trying to say?" She took her hands out of his grasp, frowning.

"There's nothing and no-one in our way anymore." He lifted her up and twirled her around exuberantly. "I'm taking you home now. We fly back this evening."

"Ugh, put me down," protested Sonja.

With her feet on the floor, she looked at him seriously. "I can't just drop everything from one minute to the next. I just can't!"

"You're so hard-working," he answered, winking at her. "Don't worry about it; I'll take care of it."

"No! I've got an appointment in a minute. I can't cancel now."

He stared at her.

Sonja pushed past him towards the corridor. "Cancel the flight. We'll talk about everything in the morning."

Robert grabbed her arm. "Sonja, please. Wait!"

"I really don't have time!" She yanked her arm away and entered the stairway.

"Just wait!" Robert hurried after her. "So you'll be a little late. The world's not going to end. You can't just leave me here like this."

He held her again. Sonja pushed him back, hard.

Robert tripped. He tried to hold on to her; he caught the pearl necklace around her neck. It broke apart with the quietest of noises.

Robert eventually lost his balance and fell, screaming, down the stairs.

THE END

The Pope's Banker

17th June 1982

It was a good thing the London evenings were still inhospitably cold, even shortly before the beginning of summer. It made it seem natural for the man to turn up the collar on his coat and pull his hat down over his forehead before he left his dosshouse.

He wandered back and forth through the streets for an hour and stopped in a couple of pubs along the way. In each one, he drank a beer at leisure whilst he gazed steadfastly out of the window and observed the people on the street. By the time he eventually reached his destination, he was convinced that nobody had followed him.

He hesitated for a moment in front of the elegant residence before reaching out his hand toward the bell. But he didn't have a choice.

As the door opened, he was faced with a young man in the dim light of the hallway. "Come in, the Monsignore is expecting you."

The man flinched. He hadn't expected to be addressed in Italian here. He eyed the stranger suspiciously.

"Come," said the stranger again and invited him into the house with a gesture of his hand.

Hesitantly, the man entered the small library in which his host was examining an old folio; a glass of wine in his hand.

"Signore, it's been brought to my attention that this time we must help you. So, what can I do for you?"

"Monsignore, I need three-hundred thousand – at least – by the end of the month."

"Three-hundred thousand what?" The old priest smiled mockingly. "Surely not lire."

The man began to feel hot in his coat. This wasn't a good start. "Dollars of course," he proclaimed. "This afternoon, I was deposed as the president of the *Banco Ambrosiano*. I can't access the accounts anymore. But Pippo Calò wants his money back."

"Really? We thought he supported our good deeds as a way of buying forgiveness for his sins."

The blatant sarcasm made the disempowered banker shudder. *Cosa Nostra* was threatening his family and this preacher was practically laughing at him. He got ahold of himself. "Only the lodge knows that the money laundering took place via the Institute for the Works of Religion. Calò thinks he's invested his money well."

"Well, in so doing he has invested his money well. If Somoza had defeated the insurrection, he'd already be able to operate freely in Central America. But now he just has to wait a while. Every investment carries certain risks."

"Very witty," remarked the banker. "The Honoured Society knows that our entire financial system has collapsed. They don't care where I get the money from – and neither do I! You're my last chance."

The priest put the folio to one side and moved slowly towards the banker. "Are you trying to blackmail me?"

"No, Monsignore; not at all. I'm just pointing out that I have no other choice anymore." The banker tried his hardest to remain polite. "I would be really sorry to cause you any difficulties."

"There's no reason for there to be any!"

"Well...," the banker considered each word carefully. "There is the possibility of problems if there were the impression that the Vatican had been financing the Contra in Nicaragua until now. And certainly, everyone understands that the Pope cares particularly about his Poland. But just as certainly, some people see the support of Solidarność as meddling with home affairs."

"The Vatican supports the churches of all poor countries."

"But the money doesn't always arrive in the parish treasuries. Perhaps tomorrow your ambassador will find this topic more appealing than you do."

"Why would the Czech ambassador be interested in Solidarność or the Contra in Nicaragua?"

They stared each other down. Both knew the answer all too well. The Czechoslovakian government couldn't tolerate an independent trade union in their neighbouring country even more than they couldn't tolerate the counterrevolution in Central America. But neither of them said a word. The crackling of the fire was the only noise for several minutes.

Then the priest nodded. The banker exhaled involuntarily. He had won.

"Signore, I'm sure you have a few interesting documents for us."

"I left them in the hotel. They're worth every cent.

"I'm sure." His host smiled and gestured towards the corner table. "Signore, you'll have a glass of wine with me before you go? My man will accompany you home afterwards. We'll take care of the necessary transactions in the morning." He turned towards the door. "Carboni, bring the Signore a glass."

The next morning, a postman found the banker hanging from underneath the Blackfriars Bridge.

The dead banker had a name: Roberto Calvi. This short story is complete speculation about what could have preceded his death.

***

Eleven years later, a Roman court sentenced the Czecho-slovak bishop Pavel Hnilica and Flavio Carboni to long prison sentences for the concealment of Calvi's briefcase. It took seven years for the bishop to be acquitted at an appeal hearing, on the grounds he became involved with Carboni in good faith. Carboni, who was involved in many scandals of the time, was not acquitted.

In May 2002, the court eventually decided that Calvi was murdered.

But who was the killer?

Not yet? THE END

***

If you enjoyed these short stories, please recommend them further. Recommendations and reviews help others to find books worth reading.

About the author:

Annemarie Nikolaus began literary writing at the beginning of 2001. After publishing many short stories, her first novel was published in 2005. She now publishes her work independently.

She was born in Hessen and lived in Northern Italy for 20 years. In 2010, she moved to Auvergne, France with her daughter.

After studying psychology, journalism, politics and history, she worked as a psychotherapist, political advisor, journalist, lecturer and translator, among others.

Blog in English: http://bit.ly/2G0ugGJ

If you would like to get in touch:
Facebook: http://www.facebook.com/AnnemarieNikolaus
Twitter: http://twitter.com/AnneNikolaus

Publications:

In English:

Magical Stories. Short stories for children. Paperback edition ISBN 9782902412600.

Radiant Hope. Illustrated science-fiction story. Paperback edition ISBN 9782902412600.

The Granddaughter. *"Quick, quick, slow - Lietzensee Dance Club"*. Paperback edition ISBN 9782902412136

Back onto the Dance Floor. *"Quick, quick, slow - Lietzensee Dance Club"*. Paperback edition ISBN 9782902412303.

Falling for a movie star. *"Quick, quick, slow - Lietzensee Dance Club"*. Paperback edition ISBN 9782902412006

Broken Rules. Historical crime short stories. Paperback edition ISBN 9782902412686

Silenced. Short thriller. Paperback edition ISBN 9782902412860

Gone... Short Stories. Paperback edition ISBN 9782902412877.

The Piratess. *"Dragon World"* series. Fantasy novel. Paperback edition ISBN 9782902412679

Aquitaine: The End of a War. *"By The Wayside..."* series. Paperback edition ISBN 9782902412808

In German:

Novels and short stories

Historical

Königliche Republik. Historical novel. Paperback edition
ISBN 9782902412471

Verjährt. Historical crime short stories. Paperback edition
ISBN 9782902412549.

Fantasy

Die Piratin. „*Drachenwelt*" series. Fantasy novel. Paperback
edition ISBN 9782902412495

Das Feuerpferd. Fantasy novel, together with Monique Lhoir
und Sabine Abel. Paperback edition ISBN 9782902412501

Magische Geschichten. Short stories for children and adults.
Paperback edition ISBN 9782902412488

Renntag in Kruschar. „*Drachenwelt*" series. Fantasy
anthology. E-Book only

Leuchtende Hoffnung. A Science Fiction novel in Advent
calendar form. Paperback edition ISBN 9782902412563

Crime and Suspense

Haus zu verkaufen. Novel. Paperback edition ISBN
9782902412983

Ustica. Short story thriller. Paperback edition ISBN
9782902412556. Paperback with voucher for the e-Book.

Tot. Short stories. Paperback edition ISBN 9782902412587.

Verjährt. (see above)

Romance

Die Enkelin. '*Quick, quick, slow - Tanzclub Lietzensee*'
series. Love story. Paperback edition ISBN 9782902412518.

Flirt mit einem Star. '*Quick, quick, slow - Tanzclub Lietzensee*' series. Love story. Paperback edition ISBN 9782902412532

Zurück aufs Parkett. '*Quick, quick, slow - Tanzclub Lietzensee*' series. Story of love and marriage. Paperback edition ISBN 9782902412525

Non-fiction

Tourist attractions

Aquitanien: Das Ende eines Krieges. '*Am Rande des Weges ...*' series. Paperback edition ISBN 9782902412570

Background series on literature and books

Suche Reisebegleitung. *Fliegende Blätter*. Paperback edition ISBN 9781499608427

Junge Welten. *Fliegende Blätter*. Paperback edition ISBN 9781500971991